HORSE DIARIES

· Darcy ·

HORSE DIARIES

HORSE DIARIES

Darcy

WHITNEY SANDERSON

illustrated by RUTH SANDERSON

RANDOM HOUSE NEW YORK

Text copyright © 2013 by Whitney Robinson
Cover art and interior illustrations copyright © 2013 by Ruth Sanderson
Photograph credit: © Bob Langrish (p. 139)

All rights reserved. Published in the United States by
Random House Children's Books, a division of Random House, Inc., New York.

Random House and the colophon are registered trademarks of Random House, Inc.

Visit us on the Web! randomhouse.com/kids

Educators and librarians, for a variety of teaching tools, visit us at
RHTeachersLibrarians.com

Library of Congress Cataloging-in-Publication Data
Sanderson, Whitney.
Darcy / Whitney Sanderson ; illustrated by Ruth Sanderson. — 1st ed.
p. cm. — (Horse diaries ; 10)
Summary: Born on a windy hill off the coast of Ireland in 1917, a Connemara pony named Darcy is sold to a farm family and trained to pull a cart and plow.
ISBN 978-0-307-97635-2 (trade) — ISBN 978-0-375-97121-1 (lib. bdg.) —
ISBN 978-0-307-97636-9 (ebook)
1. Connemara pony—Juvenile fiction. [1. Connemara pony—Fiction.
2. Ponies—Fiction. 3. Ireland—History—1910–1921—Fiction.]
I. Sanderson, Ruth, ill. II. Title.
PZ10.3.S217Dar 2013 [Fic]—dc23 2011039875

Printed in the United States of America

10 9 8 7 6 5 4 3 2 1

First Edition

To my sister, Morgan

—W.S.

For Whitney and Morgan

—R.S.

CONTENTS

"Oh! if people knew what a comfort to horses a light hand is . . ."
—from *Black Beauty*, by Anna Sewell

HORSE DIARIES
·Darcy·

Ireland, 1917

I was born in late spring, in a damp green fell that glittered with dew. My dam was a dappled-gray mare named Nessa who had worked the land for twenty years before retiring to deliver her last few foals. On the same day, sheltered from the wind by the same prickly furze hedge with its yellow flowers, another dappled-gray mare also gave birth to a black foal. My dam and the other mare, Alana, belonged to different farmers who shared the field.

The other filly was already standing by the time I pushed my way through the birthing sac and took my first gasps of salty air. My first memory is of seeing her nuzzling her dam's side to find milk. Of course I would have known what to do anyway, but from that moment onward I felt like I was following in her hoofprints.

For the first few days, everything was too strange and new for us to venture far from our dams' warm sides. But we watched each other in silent curiosity, flicking our fuzzy tails. One of the first things we learned was that the world was very wet. The air was mild, but it rained nearly every day, soaking us to the skin.

There was no shelter in our pasture except for the hedges and the ruins of a stone barracks that had lost two of its walls to the decay of time. The sea was a blue-green blur on the horizon, but the rhythmic sound of the tides filled my ears from my earliest memory.

One of the farmers had a small grandson, and he brought the boy out to visit us soon after we were born. The child's eyes were as soft and dark as those of the rabbits that darted in and out of their underground burrows, their white backsides flashing in the dusk. The boy squeezed his eyes shut when the other filly stepped forward to snuffle at the patterned fabric he wore over his bare skin instead of proper fur. I was also curious, but I was too timid to approach. The filly nipped experimentally at the collar of the boy's jacket, and he ran to hide behind his grandfather.

Yuck, said the filly, who was quite naughty and tried to taste almost everything she saw. *They aren't good to eat.*

"Both'n the babies are black," said the boy, peering from behind the old man's walking stick. "Be they twins?" Although I didn't understand

the words, I was fascinated by the lilting rise and
fall of his voice.

"No, lad. Each mare has had her own foal.
But they are a spitting image of each other, aren't
they? And do you know, Mr. Connelly said he'd
be right grateful if you'd name Alana's little
colteen as well as our Nessa's."

"Like I named Silk's kittens, Granda?"

"Just like that."

The boy was silent for a moment, gazing shyly at me. "I want to name that one Darcy," he said finally, pointing to me, "and the other one Ciara. After the twins Mam had that died before they were baptized. Is it right to do that?"

The lines on the old farmer's face seemed to grow deeper. But as he looked between me and the other filly, the ghost of a smile flickered on his face. "Aye, lad, those would be grand names. Did you know that *Ciara* and *Darcy* both mean 'dark-haired one' in the old Irish tongue?"

A misting rain had begun to fall. I was used to it, but the boy began to shiver. "We'd best be getting inside before ye catch your death of cold," said the farmer, putting a hand on the boy's shoulder.

"Won't the ponies catch cold too?"

"Nay, they thrive on the wind and the wild sea air. This land would cripple the finest Thoroughbred, but Connemara ponies are tough."

The pair traced their steps back over the hilltop. The boy bolted ahead and the old man followed at a slower pace, leaning heavily on his stick.

The other filly—Ciara—reached over and gave me a playful nip. *Race you to that clump of heather on the hill,* she said. Now that we had sorted out our legs, all she wanted to do was race. She bolted away before I could argue. I was sleepy, and I'd rather have had a nap than a run. But I couldn't help chasing after her, even though I knew I'd never catch up. Sure enough, she was already cantering toward some new adventure by the time I reached the patch of purple flowers.

That was how it always was between us.

Ciara, my shadow sister, my dark twin. Our resemblance grew as we did, and we were like mirrors of each other in a still pond. But she was the bold one, the brave one. I often felt like her timid reflection, tagging along despite my better judgment.

Ciara had a knack for finding anything prickly, precarious, or otherwise dangerous. She scaled the stone ruins as nimbly as a goat. She danced across mossy boulders that crumbled under her hooves. She plunged into tangles of blackberry thorns without a second thought, and somehow emerged without a scratch on her body.

Meanwhile, I waited at the edge of the briar patch, and licked jealously at the berry juice dripping from her muzzle. I knew from experience that if I followed her, I'd end up with a twisted fetlock or a stinging cut on my haunches. Ciara was fearless, and maybe that was what kept her in a constant state of grace.

The summer ripened to golden autumn and then faded into a gray winter. Ciara and I ventured farther and farther from our dams as we explored the limits of our pasture. In three directions it simply ended in a stone wall, but our fourth wall was the sea. We had been told many times not to get too close to the face of the cliff. Naturally, Ciara paid no attention.

One gray day, she walked to its very edge. Bits of stone crumbled beneath her hooves and fell into the ocean. I could hear the thunder of waves hitting the rocks below. The sea was beautiful, with iridescent colors that reflected the sky, but I feared its power.

Come closer, Darcy! cried Ciara as I lingered a safe distance away. *Look at the waves!*

It's not safe, I said, scraping my hoof along the ground. *Let's go find something to eat.* A large bird was circling above us, and it let out a piercing cry. I jumped, and Ciara laughed.

We're sea horses, remember? she said. When we were newly born our dams had told us that long ago there were no creatures like us on the earth. Then a great sea god had spoken magic words, and the horses came galloping out of the water.

A gust of wind and spray whipped in from the sea. Ciara reared up on her slim legs to greet it, slashing at the whirlwind with her hooves. The image burned forever in my mind, her silhouette framed against the bruised sky. She looked so wild and unafraid. Her eyes glittered, dark and full of life.

A shadow passed over us. Another bird had risen from a roost on the cliffs to join its mate. They were sea eagles with wickedly curved beaks and mottled wings that seemed to block out half the sky. They wheeled around each other, swooping and parting, but ominously silent. Then one of them made a sudden dive toward us.

My squeal of warning came too late. The bird hit Ciara's flank, leaving three red slashes, then it tumbled over the side of the cliff. Ciara was caught off guard and crashed to her knees. She thrashed to regain her footing on the slippery rock.

Then the second eagle dove. Its talons pierced Ciara's neck and held fast, its wings beating against the wind. Ciara lost her balance and fell with it over the ledge.

I could not move or make a sound. I trembled

and the earth trembled beneath me from the sea's endless assault on the cliffs. The world was suddenly empty, as if I were the only creature who had ever existed. There was a strange smell in the air that mixed with the salt and fish scent of the ocean. It was sharp and metallic. I'd smelled it before when Ciara and I had stumbled on a newly killed rabbit. It was blood.

I could not bear to look over the edge and see her body on the rocks. From below, I heard the muffled squabble of the two eagles fighting over their prey. There was nothing I could do to chase them away. I felt as helpless as a newborn foal standing for the first time. I had always looked to Ciara to know what to do, but now she was gone.

For the first time in my life, I was alone.

King Solomon's Test

My dam said it was the winter that turned our pasture cold and lifeless, but I felt like Ciara's death had drained the world of color and warmth. Alana whinnied into the wind for weeks. She bared her teeth at any creature who approached. She would not seek shelter from the wind and rain, but paced endlessly across the hills until she was worn away to nearly a skeleton.

Then one day she came over to where my dam and I were eating a pile of hay. In colder months, the farmer sometimes left us a bale at the gate. Even so, all of us were ribby from the poor foraging.

My dam sidestepped so that Alana could eat without feeling threatened, but the mare did not seem interested in the food. She was staring at me with fever-bright eyes. She stretched out her neck and whooshed a hot breath into my nostrils.

My dam flattened her ears uneasily, but Alana did not threaten or attack. Instead, she pivoted her hindquarters so I could reach her udder.

My milk has nearly dried up with no foal to nurse, she said, her voice hoarse from calling to her foal. *But grass is scarce and your milk is thin,*

Nessa. Let your filly be nourished by what little I have left to give.

My dam considered the ragged mare for a moment, then nudged me toward Alana's udder. *Many thanks, my friend.*

It was strange to suckle from a mare who was not my dam, but I was grateful for the extra food. From that day on, it was as if I had two mothers. Alana ate with us and kept watch at night to protect me from danger. I grew sleek and strong on the milk of two mares. By spring I had exceeded both of them in height. They were small, shaggy ponies who had farmed this stony soil for generations. Their ancestors had survived the Great Famine, when most of the larger horses in Ireland had died for want of feed.

One morning, when a blush of green had begun to spread across the landscape, the old farmer returned to our pasture. Another man walked with him. They seemed startled to discover only one foal, and spent hours searching the pasture for the other. But of course they found no trace of her. The wind, the sea, and the eagles had seen to that long ago.

Finally, the men returned to where I was resting on the chilly grass. My empty belly rumbled, and I rose to my feet and trotted over to my dam to nurse.

"That settles it, Connelly," said the old farmer. "'Tis my Nessa's foal."

My dam's udder was nearly dry. There was less milk every day, and my dam said it was because I was getting too grown up to nurse. But I still preferred the creamy milk to the dried grass on which the mares subsisted. I went to Alana and got a little more milk from her, then flopped back down to resume my nap.

"Perhaps 'twasn't my foal that disappeared,"

said Connelly. "But how are we to know for sure? Both mares seem to think the little one is theirs."

"Aye, but surely if we put our heads together, we can think up a test worthy of old King Solomon."

I had no idea what they meant, but if I had, I would have leaped right over the stone wall of my pasture and galloped away.

You see, as a churchgoing pony, I later learned that King Solomon was a man who settled a dispute in which two women claimed to own the same baby. He said, *Cut the baby in half, and both women shall have an equal share.* But of course the real mother said, *No, let the other woman have him, just don't hurt my child.* Thus King Solomon knew the baby belonged to that woman, and he was returned to her. Horses tied to hitching posts under stained-glass windows have learned much about the strange ways of people.

The two farmers weren't planning to cut me in half, but what they came up with wasn't much better. They returned the next day with a whole crowd of people. Everyone gathered at the fresh-water pool where we drank. Someone had brought a boat down to the water, and it was floating at the pond's bank. I hardly had a chance to take a good look at it before the old farmer whipped out a blindfold and tied it over my eyes.

Before I could object, someone prodded me in the rump with what felt like a walking stick. I scooted forward, aiming a kick behind me for good measure. My ears flicked in all directions, trying to make up for my lack of sight. Now the ground felt different under my feet. My hooves made a hollow sound, and suddenly the earth seemed to sway beneath them.

Mother? Alana? What's going on here? I whinnied. Then someone took off the blindfold and I saw for myself.

I was in a tiny boat in the middle of the pond, and the farmer Connelly was holding my lead rope. The sight of water everywhere filled me with fear, and I reared up on my hind legs. Connelly gave my hindquarters a shove, and I toppled into the water with a splash.

So that was it, I was going to drown. The cold water numbed my body, and my legs flailed helplessly, searching for solid ground. But somehow I stayed afloat as long as my legs churned. If I let them hang limp to rest, I began to sink like a stone.

My eyes were so wet and blurry that I could

hardly see better than when I was blindfolded. I heard my dam calling to me, and I swam toward the sound. My hooves hit the slimy bottom of the pond as I neared the shore. I galloped over to my mother with tendrils of seaweed streaming from my legs.

Why did they throw me in the water? I asked indignantly as my dam nosed every inch of me to make sure I hadn't been injured.

I don't know, said my dam, satisfied that I was unharmed. I heard Alana whinny, and for the first time I noticed that someone was holding her near the far shore of the pond.

"I guess we've proven the filly is yours," Connelly said gloomily as the old farmer buckled a halter over my head. "Grand big one too. Ought to fetch a fine price at auction."

My dam let out a sigh at these words.

What's the matter? I asked.

Auction, my dear, is the place where your new life begins.

You mean I must leave you and Alana? Where will I go? Will I ever see you again?

Before she could reply, the old farmer started to lead me away. My dam trailed behind us. Alana had been set loose, and she galloped over.

The farmer opened the gate. For the first time in my life, I stepped outside my pasture. The mares stood patiently and did not try to follow.

Goodbye, sweet Darcy, said Alana. *Work faithfully for your new owner.*

My dam said nothing, only watched as the farmer led me down the dusty track. I felt as if my heart were breaking—not only because I was leaving, but because they hardly seemed sad at all. I couldn't have known then that I was one of a dozen foals they had borne, and that each had been taken away to be sold. Except for Ciara, of course.

I was only a yearling then and knew little about the ways of men and farming. But my life as a free and wild creature had come to an end, and I was soon to learn.

A New Herd

The farmer brought me to a rough stone pen beside his cottage. There was no grass, and I had only an ancient donkey for company. I was fattened on oats and corn so I would fetch a good price at auction. On market day, the farmer hitched the donkey to a rickety cart, tied me to the back, and led me down the winding dirt road into town.

The street was full of carts and wagons pulled by horses of every description. Thoroughbreds pulled buggies with glinting wheels, draft horses hauled loaded hay wagons, and shaggy ponies trotted with rattletrap carts behind them. Sometimes there were as many as a dozen children crammed into the cart beds, leaning over the edges like eager puppies.

The farmer stopped in the dusty town square. There were many horses here, mostly weanlings like myself. Strange people ran their hands over my neck and haunches. They picked up my hooves and opened my mouth so they could check my teeth.

A man in a checkered cap paused to talk to

my owner, his lanky teenage son listening carefully to every word. They haggled for a minute,
then clapped each other's hands to seal the deal.
Just like that, I was sold.

My new owner handed over some coins and led me away. "This is a sturdy young filly," he said to his son. "She won't be ready to work for another year, but if you buy a weanling you know it hasn't been mistreated or worked into the ground. A mare is best for farming, because she'll keep her mind on her work and bear a colt or filly to sell each season." The man gave me a slap on the neck as he hitched me to the back of a milk delivery cart. I knew it was a friendly gesture, but I flinched. Everything was so new and strange.

"Thanks for the lift, Donovan," my new owner said to the man on the high seat of the milk cart.

"No problem, McKenna. Ye know I pass right by your place on the way home." The man glanced over his shoulder. "Looks like ye got yourself a new addition to the family."

"Aye, 'tis lucky we had a good harvest last season," said Mr. McKenna. "We haven't been able to afford a horse since old Bramble passed. Taken two years to scrape up the cash, it has. We've borrowed Elson's donkey to haul our turf, but nothing beats a Connemara pony for an honest day's work."

I had to trot to keep up with the pace of the horse pulling the milk cart. The glass jars rattled in their wooden crates. The road cut through fields that were crisscrossed by stone walls and dotted with whitewashed barns and cottages. In the distance I could see the shimmering outline of the coast. A hint of ocean smell lingered in the air, mixed with the scent of manure, grass, and soil.

For several hours I ambled in the wake of the cart. Around midafternoon, we turned from the road into a muddy barnyard. A bony cow was grazing in a field behind the barn, which was little more than a pile of stones. The nearby cottage looked the same, with the addition of a chimney that puffed gray smoke. It looked like any of a dozen other farms I had passed, but I guessed this one was mine.

I couldn't see or smell any horses aside from the draft pulling the milk cart. A pang of unease ran through me. Every horse dreads being alone, without others of its kind to groom and talk to. A horse without a herd is lost. Was I doomed to live with only a cow for company?

The teenage boy jumped down to untie me from the cart. At that moment, a woman and a small herd of children came tumbling out of the cottage. They were followed by half a dozen black-and-white balls of fluff. I reached down and nosed one curiously, for I had never seen a kitten before. The creature hissed, and I jumped back in alarm. But the kittens were not the end of the parade. Six baby geese came waddling out of the cottage and were soon pecking at my hooves.

In the midst of this confusion, a little girl started braiding ribbons into my mane. Another child held out an orange object on his palm. It was my first carrot, and it was a much more pleasant introduction than the kittens.

In the weeks that followed, I came to know the people in that unfamiliar sea of faces. Mr. McKenna and his wife had two daughters and two sons. Shannon, a girl of sixteen, was the eldest. She was beautiful, with slender white hands and a quick laugh. Her brother Liam was the lad who'd come to the auction. He was fifteen, but nearly as tall as his father. Tomas was twelve and wore funny round spectacles that made him look like an owl. Fiona, the youngest girl, was eight, and her curly red hair always seemed to be escaping from its braids.

Aside from the cow, who was rather dreamy and dull, I had the kittens, a dozen chickens, a pair of bristly pink pigs, and the geese for company. The kittens grew up to become sleek, deadly mousers, and the goslings turned into elegant, snowy-white geese. Unfortunately, they were also quite stupid. They were too tall to scramble under the pasture gate like the chickens did, so at breakfast time they all stood in a row and honked sadly because they couldn't reach the spilled grain.

Rarely were the animals shut inside for the night—only on Saturday evenings so the family could milk the cow and go to church on Sunday without fetching us from a far corner of the pasture. The rest of the time we came and went as we pleased.

When I wasn't filling my belly with sweet meadow grass, I liked to stand near the gate to watch the goings-on of the family. On sunny days, Mrs. McKenna churned butter or spun wool in the yard, and Mr. McKenna was always fixing something that had broken. When the children had a free moment from their chores, they liked to play ball games or mark out hopscotch grids in the dirt with a sharp stick. No matter how busy they were, someone always spared me a friendly pat or a leafy turnip top to crunch.

I still missed Alana and my dam, but I had found a new herd in the McKenna family.

Shannon and Fiona loved to weave colorful flowers into my mane, and I kept Tomas company in the stable while he secretly read books he had borrowed from school. The cow got milked and the pigpen mucked between chapters of *Huckleberry Finn*. If my sharp ears heard someone coming, I would snort and raise the alarm so Tomas could hide his book under a straw bale.

Liam was the quietest of the McKenna children. He worked hard beside his father in the fields, but I often saw him gazing into the distance as if he were imagining someplace far away. He was the first of the McKenna children to ride me, sneaking out of the house at night and coaxing me over to the stone wall. I was quite startled the first time he flung himself onto my back, holding tight to my mane as I raced around the pasture until I was sweaty and winded. In the morning, Mr. McKenna saw the dried flecks of foam on my chest and wondered aloud if a fox or a stray dog had spooked me in the night.

My life was certainly different now, but in some ways it was less lonely than at my home on the seacoast, where for months at a time I saw no creature other than the two mares, the birds above, and an occasional fox or rabbit. But the ache of Ciara's death never left me, and often the sight of my shadow cast on the turf or the wall of the barn reminded me of what I had lost.

Sea and Soil

Now that I was two years old, it was time for me to earn my keep. All the creatures on the farm worked for their oats: The cow gave her milk, the chickens and geese gave eggs, and the pigs . . . well, the less said about that, the better.

I had been trained to pull a cart and plow, and

my slender frame had filled out with muscle. I still stood only fourteen hands high, but my hooves were hard as flint and my coat shone with good health. My fuzzy baby fur had shed out and now I was dappled gray, with a storm-colored mane and tail.

My pasture was large enough that I could forage for most of my food, but there was always a scoop of oats waiting for me at the end of a day's work. In the mornings, Mr. McKenna hitched me to the pony cart and dropped the children off at the schoolhouse, some seven miles away. Liam and Fiona dragged their feet, muttering that they'd rather sow potatoes or gather reeds to rethatch the roof. But Tomas loved reading and sums, and Shannon treasured every opportunity to gossip with her friends.

In the misty cold days of March, my main task was hauling seaweed from the shore to fertilize the potato fields. The slimy plants were full of minerals that the stony soil lacked. But it takes a

lot of seaweed to fertilize a field, and all of it had to be carried on my back in scratchy woven baskets. The seaweed had a pungent, fishy scent that filled my nostrils so I could smell nothing else for days.

At first the smells and sounds of the seashore filled me with dread. I remembered Ciara and the eagles on the cliff. But the coast was different here, more open and gentle. The waves that skimmed to shore looked like the manes of white horses galloping in from the depths of the sea. The salty gales that whipped the coast made me feel free, even with a pannier of soggy kelp strapped to my back.

Sundays were our day of rest. The family ate a quick breakfast of boiled potatoes and hitched me up to drive the twenty miles into town. The horses, naturally, remained tethered outside the stone church. The sound of hymns and sermons drifted out through the colorful stained-glass windows.

Sunday mornings were the perfect opportunity to catch up on the latest gossip. We farm ponies rarely stepped off our own land during the week. If we did, we were too busy to stop and socialize. While our families worshiped, we had ample time to shoot the breeze about the growth of crops, new foals, or the goings-on at Hulton Manor.

Sir Henry Hulton was the main landowner in this part of the county. The McKennas leased their farm from Sir Henry, and they had to pay most of their earnings to him. Since the rent was so high, few farmers could save enough money to buy the land that they worked.

The other ponies claimed that the Hultons owned the finest Thoroughbreds in all of Connemara. These fabled horses slept in stalls the size of entire cottages that were bedded with goose down. They wore silver horseshoes and ate oats mixed with molasses three times a day.

It sounded like a tale as tall as an evening shadow to me. My life was certainly nothing like that. Indeed, by the time May wildflowers bloomed, the hardest labor of all began. Wood was scarce near the rocky coast, and people in Connemara relied on turf bricks to heat their cottages. The McKennas harvested their turf from the peat bog that lay between their farm and the town.

The bog was a vast expanse of puddles and waterlogged earth. The ground sucked at my hooves and swallowed any object that was set down and forgotten. People used heavy spades to cut the turf into bricks, which were then stacked to dry in the sun.

One of my jobs was to carry these blocks of earth back to the McKenna farm, so they would have fuel enough to last the winter. It was hard work, but I thrived on it. The other farmers made envious comments when they saw how lightly I pulled a full cartload of turf.

I was impervious to the wind and cold, and I rarely sought shelter in the barn. I felt sorry for the humans, who had no fur to protect them from the elements. On the other hand, they could take off their clothes to dry them. It rained more days than not, and my coat was usually damp beneath my harness. Sometimes the leather rubbed my fur right off and made a sore. When that happened, Mr. McKenna was quick to apply a salve of goose grease to the wound.

On afternoons when I didn't have other work to do, Fiona and Tomas would often go to the beach to collect mussels, riding double on my back. Even on cloudy days the water was a brilliant

turquoise color. While one child waded in the shallows with a bucket, the other would find a stretch of smooth white sand to gallop on.

And so my first year with the McKennas passed more quickly than I could have imagined. I rarely thought of my old life now. I had grown to love all the McKenna children, and my days were spent in a joyful harmony of work and play. But outside the sheltered hills of our farm, things were changing.

Ireland was at war. I didn't know what that meant, but it seemed to be all people talked about. War and freedom. To me, freedom was being let out of my harness after a day of plowing so I could have a good roll in the dirt.

One afternoon when I was sowing furrows for seed potatoes, I noticed a line of men marching down the road toward town. I would have heard the tramp of feet sooner, but Mr. McKenna was singing as he worked. My ears were filled with "Black is the color of my true love's hair" and "Red is the rose that in yonder garden grows."

The men were nearly in front of our noses by the time we noticed them. They were all dressed in the same round hats and long jackets with brass buttons. Some were walking, and others were riding in a cart behind a pair of stocky bay horses.

They carried rifles, but this wasn't so unusual. Mr. McKenna sometimes took me out to hunt rabbits and grouse in the brushy lowlands. I didn't like the gun's sharp report, or the smell of burning that lingered in the air, but I'd gotten used to it. Still, it seemed strange that so many men would be walking down our road, carrying guns.

There were more of them than there were rabbits to eat, I was certain.

Strangest of all was Mr. McKenna's reaction to this odd parade. He stopped in his tracks and his voice died on his lips. If I hadn't had to wait when I reached the end of the furrow, I could have plowed the world's longest seed potato row. One of the soldiers raised a hand to Mr. McKenna as they passed, but he didn't return the greeting. When the troop had marched out of sight, Mr. McKenna returned to the plow. His face was grim, and he seemed to have forgotten the rest of his song.

Black and Tans

Soon after the soldiers came, the family made a trip into town. The McKennas grew most of their food and had little extra to spare. Much of their rent to the Hultons was paid in the form of grain. Instead of cash, the McKennas brought eggs, milk, wool, and homemade jams to trade for shop credit.

When the family pulled up in front of Beadle's General Store and Apothecary, Liam said he
would wait outside. Fiona, Tomas, and Shannon
followed their parents into the store. Through the
window I could see that Shannon was dabbing
samples of rouge onto her cheeks and spraying
herself with amber liquid from a crystal bottle.

Tomas and Fiona went straight for the candy
jars lining the walls. Their lips moved soundlessly
as they argued about how many root beer barrels,
lemon drops, and licorice sticks should fill the
small bag they would get to share as a treat. This
was a topic that interested me as well, for Fiona
could always be counted upon to slip me a candy
for the drive home.

A pair of British soldiers were loitering outside
the pub across the street, smoking and looking

bored. Their rifles, tipped with shining bayonet points, were propped up beside them. I'd heard from the ponies at church that the soldiers had taken over the Gallagher estate, which rivaled the Hultons' in size and grandeur. Brandishing their weapons, the soldiers had scarcely given the family time to pack their things.

Now the uniformed men stalked around town searching for "suspicious activity"—evidence of the Irish Republican Army, who wanted to throw the British troops out of Ireland and let the Irish rule themselves. Otherwise, the soldiers seemed mostly to occupy themselves in the pub, sometimes shooting at stray dogs and demanding "taxes" of whiskey, meat, or fruit from local shopkeepers.

I felt the cart jiggle as Liam kicked restlessly at the baseboard. I noticed that the soldiers across the street were looking in our direction. One of them crushed out his cigarette, then flicked it into the road. The cart bounced. Liam had jumped down and was approaching the soldiers.

"Ye aren't supposed to throw trash on the street," said Liam, his eyes narrowed.

The soldiers looked surprised for a moment, then laughed. "And who made you the king of County Galway, little lad?"

"Ye don't belong here," said Liam, his fingers curling into fists. "Our land was clean and good before ye came."

One of the soldiers looked annoyed, but the other reached down and picked up the cigarette with a good-natured grin. He dropped it into an empty bottle that was resting between the two men. "Happy now?" he said.

"I was talking about ye," said Liam. "Ye're trash, and ye don't—"

The first soldier grabbed his rifle and aimed it at Liam's chest. There were only a few inches of space between the muzzle and the faded plaid of Liam's shirt. I couldn't see Liam's face, but he had quickly fallen silent.

"Come on now, Keppler, he's only a boy . . . ," said the other soldier, looking uncomfortable.

"Old enough to face the firing squad," muttered the soldier with the rifle. "Hands up, little Paddy. . . ."

I didn't like this situation at all. I wanted to go over to Liam, but my reins had been tied to a post.

Just then, Shannon trotted out the door of the general store. She was smiling and gazing at a small gold tube in her hand. Her grin faded when she saw her brother facing off with the soldiers. She glanced back at the store, then hurried over to where Liam stood sullenly at gunpoint.

"What's going on here?" she said in a honey-sweet tone. "What fool thing has my brother done now?"

"Talking treason, he is," said the soldier, giving Liam a prod with the muzzle of the gun.

Shannon stepped in front of Liam and put her hand on the barrel of the rifle, flashing a coquett-ish smile that showed off her even white teeth. "He's just a hothead. Don't listen to a thing he says."

The sneer faded a little from the soldier's lips, but he still didn't lower the gun.

"Fetching lass, in't she?" said his companion,

elbowing him in the ribs. "Guess there's some benefits to being out here in the sticks. . . ."

"Aye, I reckon that English girls aren't very pretty compared to us native *savages*," said Shannon pertly, hiding the fear that I saw lingering deep in her blue eyes. "Come on, Liam," she said, grabbing her brother by the back of his collar. "Time to go."

No one argued with Shannon when she had that expression on her face. I'd seen it a thousand times—be it Shannon's turn to milk the cow or fill the pigs' slop bucket or not, you could bet that a little brother or sister would be doing the task instead. The soldier let his gun drift down, looking a bit perplexed, and Shannon marched Liam back across the street.

"What were you *thinking*?" she hissed, all but

shoving her brother into the cart. "You don't go mouthing off to the Black and Tans. They've shot people for less."

I had a feeling she was just warming up, but the rest of the family emerged from the store with their packages and Shannon fell silent. The soldiers had gone into the nearby pub. Mr. and Mrs. McKenna didn't seem to notice anything was amiss as they loaded their supplies into the back of the cart. Fiona gave me a strange-tasting pink candy.

"I don't think Darcy likes watermelon," she said to Tomas as I curled my lip at the unfamiliar treat. The two of them kept up a steady stream of chatter on the way home.

"I can't believe ye bought *lipstick* instead of candy with the money from all the bramble jam ye sold at the church fair," Tomas said to Shannon.

"Who are ye planning to kiss with yer pretty red lips—Darcy?"

I flicked back my ears at the sound of my name, and the two youngest children dissolved into giggles. Back at the farm, I settled down to an evening of grazing and soon put the afternoon's unpleasantness out of my mind.

But late that night my keen ears picked up the sound of footsteps crossing the yard. I trotted over and caught sight of a silhouette heading toward the road. Horses' eyes are quite sharp at night, and I realized it was Liam with his school knapsack slung over his shoulder.

I whinnied to him, but he did not turn. Where could he be going at such an hour? I called to him again and he hesitated, then hurried over to the fence.

"Hush, Darcy," he said, putting his hand on my muzzle. "Ye'll wake everyone."

I nosed at him curiously. I smelled bread in his bag and hoped he might share. But he only gave me an absent pat, then whispered, "Be good, sweet Darcy. I wish I could ride ye to Dublin instead of sneaking onto a railway car like a common tramp. But it's unfair to bring beasts into men's wars, and 'twould be as bad as stealing to leave Ma and Da without a horse. Take care of them, will ye?"

Liam's hand tightened briefly on the bridge of my nose, then let go. He turned and slipped away into the night, my eyes tracking his progress until he was swallowed by darkness.

English Roses

In the weeks that followed, everyone moved about in a state of shock. Liam had left a note saying that he had taken the train to Dublin to join the Irish Republican Army. The family was devastated. Not only had Mr. McKenna been counting on Liam to cut extra turf to sell in town—the rent had increased again this year—but there was also a very real possibility that Liam could be killed in the brutal trench warfare between the Nationalists and the British troops.

But Liam wasn't the only McKenna child who had been harboring a secret. Shannon often took me on long rides through the countryside, saying she was going out to pick berries. But instead of going south toward the burren, where blackberries clustered like gems on the vine, she only gathered from the sparse bushes alongside the road, then continued on to Hulton Manor. She liked to gaze at the elegant house with its walled courtyard and gardens full of exotic plants.

"How wonderful it would be to own such a home," she murmured one afternoon as I paused to graze at the crest of the hill overlooking the estate. "Feather beds, great halls that sparkle with mirrors and crystal, tea served on china plates by servants every afternoon."

Shannon did her work without complaint at home, churning butter, washing clothes, and digging in the vegetable garden, but I knew she yearned for a life of refinement. At church picnics she cast envious glances at the fashionable dresses and high-heeled shoes of the town girls, daughters of shopkeepers and middle-class landowners. The Hultons themselves, like all the wealthiest people in the region, went to a different church.

As Shannon watched an old gardener pruning the maze of hedges surrounding the house, I caught the scent of a strange horse. A moment later, a young man emerged from the walled courtyard, mounted on a chestnut stallion.

No, *chestnut* wasn't the right word. The horse's coat had an almost metallic sheen. It was brighter than copper, redder than brass. I whinnied a greeting, and the stallion's hawklike head turned toward me. His nostrils flared, but he made no sound.

His rider had seen us too and urged the stallion toward us. Shannon shifted uneasily on my back, as if she wasn't sure whether to stand her ground or turn and flee.

As the pair approached, I could see that the stallion was several hands taller than me. His rider was about Shannon's age. The young man removed his hat and greeted her politely. His stallion stared at me, jingling his bit, but remained silent. I pawed uneasily at the ground.

"I—I was just admiring your gardens," said

Shannon, tugging sharply on my reins to make me stand still.

"Really? Then why don't you come take a closer look at them." The boy turned his horse and gestured invitingly. Shannon nudged me with her heels, and we followed them down the hill.

"Are you Brendan Hulton?" she asked.

"Yes. I'm recently home from Oxford." He turned in the saddle and looked us over. "And you, clearly, are some fairy maiden who has wandered accidentally into civilization."

Shannon let out a nervous and uncharacteristic giggle. "Not hardly," she said. "My family is McKenna. Your father owns our land."

We passed under a rose trellis into the garden. The hedges had been planted in a lattice pattern, like strips of pastry on top of a pie. The diamond-shaped mounds of earth in the center were filled with flowers and fruit trees. In the very middle of the garden was a fountain with water spouting from the mouth of a stone cupid. I was thirsty, and I tried to drag Shannon toward it. She dug in her heels and hissed, "Darcy, behave!"

As she and Brendan dismounted and walked together among the rows of bright blossoms, I eyed the red stallion beside me. He looked bored as he strolled beside his owner, and truth be told, I was a little insulted by his indifference. Was I not a mare, after all?

What is your name? I asked finally.

Embarr, he said, pricking his ears briefly in my direction.

Is it true that the horses here wear silver shoes? I had to ask.

Embarr pawed the air with one foreleg. Something glinted on the bottom of his hoof. *It's not silver,* he said, *but some other metal. It's not for decoration. It helps to keep our hooves from cracking when we jump cross-country.*

This sounded odd to me. I had been roaming these hills my whole life and my hooves had never cracked. By now, our owners had completed a circuit of the garden and were standing together under the rose trellis. Brendan reached up and broke the stem of the largest flower.

"An English rose for an Irish beauty," he said, handing it to Shannon with a smile. Then he glanced over at the manor house. "But I'm afraid I must be going. I'm supposed to go hunting with my father after tea, and he hates to be kept waiting. Perhaps I'll see you again?"

"Aye, perhaps," said Shannon, twirling her flower. Brendan mounted Embarr and rode across the smooth green lawn. Shannon turned me toward home in a daze. It was a good thing I knew the way, for I probably could have walked straight

into a ravine and she wouldn't have stopped sniff-
ing that rose.

When we reached the farm, an unsettling
scene awaited us. Mr. and Mrs. McKenna were
in the yard, talking to a young man in uniform.
Mrs. McKenna clutched her husband's arm, tears
streaming down her face.

Shannon jumped off my back before I had
even halted. The rose from Brendan fell from her
hands and landed by my hooves. "What is it?"
she said, hurrying over to her parents. "What's
the matter?"

"Liam," said Mr. McKenna. His face was ashen.
"He's been shot."

Night Ride

Mr. McKenna left for the train station that very evening. Liam was in a hospital in Dublin. He was still alive, but his leg had been blown off by artillery and he'd lost a lot of blood. He was in surgery now, but no one knew if he'd live.

Shannon insisted on going too. At first Mr.

McKenna had argued, saying that Dublin was no place for a young lady in these times. But as usual, Shannon managed to get her way. They rode to the station with a neighbor who had business in town, leaving Tomas and Fiona to look after the farm. Mrs. McKenna had taken to bed with a fever, and the normally squabbling siblings were unusually serious, dividing up the chores between them.

Although there was better grazing on the far side of my pasture, I stayed near the house to keep an eye on things. The day after Mr. McKenna and Shannon left for Dublin, Mrs. McKenna came outside to work in the garden despite the children's protests. "I cannot bear to stay in bed all day," she said. "When the hands are idle, the mind is full of worried thoughts." She pulled carrots and beets up by their leafy tops while Tomas and Fiona washed the supper dishes inside.

Mrs. McKenna noticed me watching her and lumbered over with a carrot in her hand. Halfway across the yard she stopped and swayed, as if the ground had turned to tossing sea beneath her feet. The carrot dropped from her hand, and she crumpled onto the ground. A red stain was spreading across the apron of her dress.

I knew that something must be terribly wrong with the baby inside her. I whinnied in alarm and struck the metal gate of my pasture with my hoof. Tomas and Fiona emerged from the cottage, drawn by the noise. They ran over to where their mother was lying on the grass. They shook her shoulders and called out to her, but she did not awaken.

"We must get a doctor," said Fiona. She ran

into the barn and emerged with my bridle. "Stay with Mother," she said to Tomas. "Fetch some water, and help her inside if she wakes up."

"But it's nearly two hours' ride into town!" said Tomas. "Ye'll never make it before nightfall. And Mother could die before then. . . ." His lip trembled.

"She won't. Darcy will gallop so fast, we'll be there in no time at all." Fiona bridled me and jumped onto my bare back. Tomas held open the gate, and Fiona dug her heels into my ribs. I sensed her urgency and broke into a gallop.

The road to town snaked away into the distance, and I remembered how long it took to drive to church each Sunday. Fiona must have thought the same thing, for she drew me to a halt and turned to face the bog that lay between the McKennas' farm and the town. The reason that the road was so circuitous was that it wound around the large expanse of swamp. Any pathway through it would simply sink into the spongy ground.

The sun blazed low on the horizon, casting twisted shadows across the bog. The land looked black and the water silver, like a mirror reflecting the burning sky. In daylight, it was hard to tell where the water ended and the earth began, because everything was the same muddy color. Now it looked like an image from a dream or a fairy tale, not like an ordinary stretch of land that could be crossed by a mortal horse.

But town was so much closer this way—less than two miles straight through, compared to twenty by the road. Fiona had made up her mind.

She urged me forward into the gloom. After a moment's hesitation, I stepped off the road. I wondered if we would ever find it again.

The most treacherous thing about the bog was that ground that appeared solid might be soft as cornmeal mush underfoot. There were ridges of safe, dry land between the pools, but sometimes they petered out and left no other way through.

As dusk gathered around us, all my senses focused on finding a safe path. My eyes were fixed on the ground, searching out hummocks of grass that signaled drier ground. My ears flicked in all directions, listening for danger. I could even smell the difference between the soil under the grass hummocks and the rich, decaying smell of the mud pits.

Fiona murmured words of encouragement from time to time, but my eyes were sharper than

hers at night, and she let me pick my own way through the gloom.

When we reached the center of the swamp, I felt a moment of disorientation. On this low ground, I could no longer see the far edge of the swamp, nor the path back to the road from which we'd come. I had only my instinct to guide me. I

knew where the town was in the same way that a bird knows how to find its way home in the spring.

The moon came out from behind a cloud, illuminating a trail through the silvery surface of a flooded plain. And beyond it was the most welcome sight I'd ever seen—a grassy bank and a glimpse of the road that led into town.

In my haste to reach it, I stopped paying such careful attention to where I stepped. I felt my hooves sink into deep mud. I tried to turn back, but the soft earth sucked at my legs and held them fast. Panicked, I thrashed deeper into the deadly sinkhole. Fiona's fingers clenched my mane, and black muck splashed her bare legs.

I had sunk up to my belly now. My instinct was to fight my way through the mud with brute strength. But if I did, Fiona could fall and be hurt. I had to get both of us out safely. Instead of stumbling deeper into the bog, I carefully lifted one of my submerged hind hooves. If I moved with aching slowness, the mud did not trap them. Only if I struggled did it bind me.

One painstaking step at a time, I backed out of the pit. It went against my every impulse, and my fear was multiplied by Fiona's trembling hands as she clenched the reins. A step, and another, and more precious time ticking away. If only we had taken the road—perhaps we were already too late to save Mrs. McKenna and her baby.

Another step, and yet another. Now the ground felt solid under my hooves. Summoning the last of my strength, I backed the rest of the way out of the pit and then followed the raised path out to the road. Any passerby who saw us emerge from the bog would probably think they'd seen the dreaded kelpie or dullahan of ancient lore.

Mud splattered from my legs and haunches as I galloped into town, but that didn't matter now. We had reached the doctor. Fiona pounded at the door, and a light went on inside the house.

8

A Matter of Honor

With the aid of Dr. Farber, who hitched his black mare and followed us back to the farm, by the road this time, Mrs. McKenna delivered a baby boy. Her fever had caused the birth to come early, but the child was healthy.

When Mrs. McKenna brought him outside for

the first time, he seemed scarcely bigger than a wild rabbit, his skin all wrinkled and pink. He grew quickly, though, and was soon brought to church to be baptized. He was named Connor, after Mrs. McKenna's father, who had left to find work in America when she was a little girl.

Meanwhile, Mr. McKenna and Shannon had returned from Dublin with Liam. I was shocked to see him balancing on two crutches, his right leg missing up to the knee. His pants were rolled up and pinned so that the fabric wouldn't drag on the ground.

He seemed to have lost something else as well. He reminded me of a corn husk after it had been stripped from the ear. His skin was sallow, and his eyes looked lifeless. I neighed to him in greeting as he crossed the yard, but he didn't even look up.

He nearly fell when his crutch hit a rock, but he shrugged off Shannon's hands with a sharp word when she tried to help him.

Once he was inside, he stayed there. He didn't go to church with the family or play outside with the younger children. It was like the boy I remembered had never returned. Only a ghost had come home to take his place.

But life went on for the rest of the McKenna family. Shannon continued her trysts with Brendan at Hulton Manor. Often she rode with him while he was out flying his falcon or jumping cross-country with Embarr. I had to admit, the stallion was a fine hunter—he could clear a five-foot hedge without a drop of sweat marring his chestnut coat. Embarr was always polite when we met, dipping his finely sculpted head in greeting and matching his sweeping strides to my short, quick ones. But there was something remote and even disdainful about his manner. It was as if he thought it beneath him to mix with a mere farm pony like myself.

One afternoon, our riders led us side by side through the magnificent walled garden at Hulton Manor. The pear trees were in bloom, and I nosed eagerly for fallen fruit when Shannon paused to rest on a stone bench. I had gobbled five or six before I noticed that Embarr was watching me with an expression of amusement. Embarrassed, I sidled away from the tree and wiped my dripping muzzle against my foreleg. Embarr, of course, was too dignified to be interested in the pears. He stood like a bronzed statue, awaiting Brendan's next command.

But Brendan had other things on his mind. He and Shannon were sitting together on the bench, holding hands. Brendan was describing some fancy ball he was going to attend that evening.

"I can't imagine what it would be like to go to such a dance," breathed Shannon, leaning closer to him. Her voice was always so small and mouselike when she spoke to him. It wasn't like her at all.

"You're a farmer's daughter," said Brendan. "What would you wear? I'd invite you myself so you could see what it's like, but I'd be a laughingstock among my school friends."

Shannon stood up. Her cheeks were flushed with anger. "Brendan Hulton, are you saying that you'd be ashamed to be seen in public with me?"

Brendan looked almost confused. "Of course," he said. "My father expects me to make friends within my own social class. Furthermore, you're a Catholic. You can't possibly think we could ever *court* each other."

For a moment, I thought Shannon was going to slap Brendan. Instead, she spun on her heel and grabbed my reins. Sensing her agitation, I took a step forward. She yanked at the reins, and I tossed my head in surprise. Shannon was usually a gentle rider.

Brendan grabbed my bridle and held me still while she mounted. I didn't like how he was upsetting Shannon, and I nipped at his hand.

"If you don't understand what I mean," he said, rubbing his wrist where I'd bitten him, "just look at our two horses. That's the difference between us."

"Oh, so I'm just a common workhorse, am I?"

Shannon's voice was far from mouselike now. It was more like the screech of an angry hawk. "I'll have you know that Darcy is the fastest and bravest horse in the county, maybe in all of Ireland."

Brendan laughed. "If you were a gentleman, I'd challenge you to a race. As it is, I can only apologize if my words have offended a lady."

"Oh, keep your stuffy words!" cried Shannon. "You don't think I'm a lady, so don't pretend to treat me like one. In fact, I *do* challenge you to a race. With a proper prize if you should win. Anything you like."

"What if I asked for a kiss?"

Shannon's cheeks burned red. "Fine, if that's what you want. But you'll never collect it."

"And you?" said Brendan. "What prize would you claim should that ill-tempered beast of yours cross the finish line first? Although I think it likelier that she would sprout wings and flap away."

"I want nothing from you," said Shannon, "except to see the look on your face when Darcy and I leave you in the dust."

Brendan's eyes flashed. His face was equally flushed, and in his expression I read hostility, amusement, and something else I could not name. How complex humans' faces are, and I believe they show only half of what is in their hearts.

"Saturday morning, two weeks hence," he said. "We begin at the manor house and end at the church steeple, a distance of some twenty miles. Embarr is a turf racer, accustomed to no more than a two-mile track, so here we shall yield the advantage to that pony of yours, who may possess some measure of stamina in those stubby legs."

I swished my tail uneasily as Shannon's fingers tightened around the reins, and Embarr let out a loud snort. I looked at him in surprise, for usually he maintained a lofty silence.

You don't think that girl of yours is the first that Brendan has tried to lure with a pretty flower, do you? he said as Shannon and Brendan shook hands to seal the wager. *Believe me, I've endured many a ride with a pretty peasant girl and her scruffy nag. I don't mean you, of course—as the local stock goes, you're really quite fetching. Perhaps there's some Arabian in your bloodlines.*

I ground my teeth and just barely restrained myself from biting a chunk out of his perfect neck. *There's nothing of the kind,* I said shortly. *I'm a Connemara pony, born and bred.*

Oh, too bad, said Embarr. I laid back my ears

and snapped at him, but my teeth hit against the bit as Shannon turned me toward the garden gate.

"We shall see you on Saturday, two weeks hence," she called over her shoulder as we cantered toward home.

"I'll have my kiss yet!" Brendan called after her. I felt her give a little flounce as she no doubt tossed her golden hair over her shoulder. I still could not tell whether they were truly angry with each other or were only playing at fighting as colts and fillies do.

But for the next week, I had hardly a moment to ponder Shannon's bet, for some government men had come with a potato sprayer for the farmers to share. Years ago, a terrible blight had caused most of the potatoes in Ireland to rot, and many people had starved. Now people planted different kinds of potatoes and coated the fields with blue-stone, a mixture of lime and water, to kill the deadly fungus. But everyone feared that the crops would rot anyway, and the months between first planting and the midsummer harvest were tense.

I spent many long afternoons trudging up and down the ridges of potato beds with the barrel full of bluestone rattling behind me. Several of our neighbors were too poor to keep a pony, and

Mr. McKenna loaned me out to help spray their fields as well.

"There is nothing more important than preventing the blight from returning," he said to Tomas, whom he was teaching how to do a man's work on the farm. Tomas looked like he'd rather be reading a book in the cool house. "My own grandparents had to leave the country and find work in America or else starve," said Mr. McKenna. "They left my father to be raised by *his* grandparents, as many families did. Ireland was a broken country for a full generation—only now that the railroads are spreading has some small measure of wealth returned to the country."

During the week my mind was occupied only with work, but on Sunday I discovered that the news of Shannon's bet with Brendan had spread like wildfire. The Hultons were not popular with the townsfolk. They were fair landlords, but snobbish and condescending. Not to mention that their Thoroughbreds often beat the stuffing out of the farm horses at local race meets, where common folk and gentry raced side by side.

When Shannon's parents got wind of the race, Mrs. McKenna tried to forbid Shannon to go through with it. "'Tis unseemly behavior for a young lady of yer age to be gallivanting about the countryside on horseback," she said as Shannon unhitched me from the cart after church, replacing my harness with a bridle so we could go for a conditioning gallop.

Mrs. McKenna looked even more tired than usual with little Connor kicking in her arms. I often heard him crying at night, and I knew nobody was getting much sleep. "Ye are nearing an age when ye ought to be thinking of hearth and home," she said to Shannon. "What respectable man would marry a young lady who spends her day galloping after the wayward sons of the gentry?"

"With any luck I'll be galloping in *front* of him, Mother," said Shannon patiently, turning me in a tight circle to stretch my neck and shoulders. "Besides, it's a matter of honor. The Hultons think so little of us tenants, and treat us as if we were muck they've scraped from their fancy boots."

"Can't argue with that," said Mr. McKenna, who was repairing a worn place in the thatched roof of the cottage. "I say let the girl race. People may talk, but times are changing. And the

Hultons have never done us any favors, all these years. I wouldn't mind seeing that lad taken down a peg."

Liam, who was sitting near the door and braiding dried marsh reeds into lengths of rope, gave me a skeptical look. "Do ye really think Darcy can match Embarr?" he said. "They say he's unbeatable at track meets. Darcy's game, but she's no racehorse."

"She is the cleverest pony in Connemara," said Shannon simply, and headed me toward the road. I leaped into a canter, then stretched out my legs until we were outracing the wind as it blew dark banks of storm clouds in from the sea. In that moment, I felt like nothing in the world could keep pace with my flight.

Match Race

The day of the race dawned clear and bright. I had gotten used to the gray blanket of clouds that normally covered the sky, but its pure blue seemed like a good omen. I was in fine condition after daily gallops in the deep sand at the beach, and was bursting with energy from a twice-daily ration of oats. Indeed, as Shannon and I headed across the hills for Hulton Manor, I could hardly keep from prancing like a carousel horse.

"Save your energy for the race, Darcy," said Shannon, reining me in.

The rest of the McKennas had hitched a ride into town with a neighbor so they could see me cross the finish line. Everyone in the county knew about the race, and more than a few shillings had been placed on its outcome.

"Ye'd better whip that young dandy and his stallion," one of the Hulton maids whispered to Shannon when we reached the manor. "Show him that our Irish ponies can run circles around their fluff-headed English Thoroughbreds. Ye know, Embarr is so spoilt that he won't eat a mash of mere oats for breakfast like the other horses.

Nay, he must have an apple cut into his feed every morning to appeal to his sensitive palate."

Shannon laughed, and I took strength in the confidence of her voice as she replied, "We shall pass the church steeple before Brendan finds his way out to the road."

"I hope so," said the maid, "for I have a day's wages riding on the back of yer mare." The girl took a ripe red apple from her apron pocket and

offered it to me. "'Tis Embarr's," she said with a giggle as I bit into the apple. "But I don't think he'll miss one, for he has been stuffed with so many that he's practically a dumpling."

Embarr, however, was in top form. He was leaner than usual, and the muscles of his neck and haunches were more defined. His copper coat gleamed as though the rays of the sun had set it on fire. Indeed, my heart sank as a stable boy led him over to where Brendan was chatting with several gentlemen in stately black suits and their ladies, who wore fashionable short dresses.

Brendan himself was clad in the strangest getup of all: buff breeches with flared hips, stiff knee-high boots, and a black jacket whose tails reached nearly to his knees. He tapped a riding crop imperiously against his palm as he spoke to the fawning crowd around him. The day was warm, and he was already sweating under his starched collar.

Brendan and Shannon lined us up outside the manor gates. Brendan coolly wished Shannon luck, and she replied that she would not need it. I felt dwarfed standing beside Embarr. To my surprise, he touched his nose briefly to mine, a friendly gesture, before Brendan tugged the reins to make him face forward.

The Hulton groundskeeper raised a pistol and fired into the air—we were off!

At first I was startled by how easy it was to keep pace with Embarr. I took two strides for every one of his, but I stuck to his side like a shadow. For several miles we ran neck and neck.

Then I noticed that Embarr wasn't sweating,

and his nostrils were hardly flared. My coat was already soaked through, and I snorted with exertion each time my hooves hit the ground. Embarr's dark eyes flashed in amusement, and suddenly I realized that he wasn't extending himself at all.

I think I'm warmed up now, said Embarr as we rounded a bend in the road. *It's been lovely, but . . .*

Embarr changed leads with a skip and surged ahead, his long legs flashing like pistons. I was literally left in his dust—it filled my lungs, choking me, and the grit stung my eyes. Shannon urged me on, but by now we both realized that I was no match for a sixteen-hand Thoroughbred.

Unless . . .

I looked over at the forbidding expanse of bog that I had traversed with Fiona. I still remembered the way through, and I didn't think I would get stuck again. Embarr was a hundred paces ahead by now, and I knew there was no chance of my catching him.

Shannon cried out in surprise as I cut sideways into the bog. She struggled to turn me back toward the road, but I held my head high to evade the bit. Then she let out a laugh and seemed to understand. She released the reins and urged me on.

By now, Brendan had noticed our shortcut and he sent the stallion chasing after us. A stone wall separated them from the bog, but they cleared it in an effortless leap. In a few of Embarr's ground-swallowing strides, they had caught up to us. But the turf was uneven, and Embarr stumbled and fell behind again.

Horses can see in nearly a full circle around

them, so even as we proceeded through the bog at a careful trot, I could see Embarr lashing his tail in frustration because he could not find his footing on the rough ground. Brendan was kicking him, trying to make him gallop to catch up with me.

With neither of them paying attention to the shifting terrain, Embarr splashed into a pool of murky water and sank nearly to his girth. Brendan, unprepared for the sudden stop, catapulted over the horse's head and landed facedown in the muck.

Shannon swiveled at the sound of Brendan's cries. She reined me to a halt, perhaps wondering if she should stop to help. But Embarr heaved himself free from the puddle. Dripping, he minced his way back toward the road, ears

flattened against his head in disgust. Brendan—
whose buff breeches I feared would never be
the same—chased after him, waving his broken
riding crop.

Shannon and I pressed onward. I edged cautiously along the trail I'd taken to reach the doctor, careful to keep my weight over my hindquarters in case the path collapsed. I lifted my hooves high over brambles and sedge and skirted around gaping mud pits. Before I knew it, we were clear of the bog and galloping onward into town. As we swept past the church steeple, we were greeted by cheers from the townsfolk and startled gasps from Sir Henry and his friends.

Shannon halted me swiftly and swung down from my back. The younger McKenna children showered me with pats and praise. Mrs. McKenna looked both vexed and proud as Shannon spun a dramatic retelling of the race to her siblings and friends who gathered around us.

It was a good half hour before Brendan and

Embarr joined the festivities. They were coated in muck from tip to tail, and Embarr was favoring his left foreleg.

Are you all right? I called. Despite the stallion's arrogance, I was sorry he'd been injured.

Only a stone bruise, said Embarr, wrinkling his nose as a drop of mud oozed from his wet forelock. *I say, it's rough country out there. Not my cup of tea, but you seemed to handle it well. Good show, indeed.*

He plunged his nose into a bucket of water someone had brought, and I thought that perhaps I had misjudged Embarr. Unfortunately, I couldn't say the same of his owner.

Brendan dismounted and stalked over to Shannon. "You cheated!" he said. "We were to race by the road, not through some infernal swamp."

Before Shannon could reply, Liam broke in.

"The race was from Hulton Manor to the church steeple," he said. "There was nothing about the track ye had to take to get here. Our pony outclassed yer fancy hunter, and that's all there is to it."

Brendan tossed Embarr's reins to a waiting servant and peeled off his mud-encrusted jacket. Unfortunately, the shirt beneath wasn't much cleaner, and the ripe scent of the peat bog drifted toward me.

"Well, I suppose she's got a certain talent for scrabbling over rocks," he said stiffly. "But she'd never have won on a fair track, and she's quite a common-looking thing."

"Ye just can't stop yer tongue a-flapping even after ye've lost, can ye?" muttered Liam, scuffing the tip of one crutch angrily in the dirt.

"Calm yourself," said Brendan with one of his

ironic smirks. "I was speaking of the horse, not your sister."

Liam dropped one crutch and delivered a solid punch to Brendan's smug face. The young aristocrat reeled back in shock, then fished frantically in his jacket for a handkerchief as his nose began to drip blood. Instead of returning the blow, he sputtered something about poor country manners and retreated hastily to his father's carriage. Several young ladies hurried over to comfort him, offering their own handkerchiefs and bringing cups of ice from the grocer.

As for Liam, he was quickly hailed by a dozen farmers offering to buy him a pint. But he refused them all and took my lead rope from Shannon, saying that he'd walk me until I was cool. She hugged him and whispered, "Thank ye! I wanted to smack him myself, but Mother would never have forgiven me!"

Nearby, I saw Mr. McKenna stiffen as Sir Henry approached.

"I apologize for my son's behavior," said Mr. McKenna in a rush, stumbling over his words. "He's recently back from the war, and he hasn't been quite himself. . . ."

"Never mind," said Sir Henry, waving a walking stick with a gold top shaped like a horse's head. "Boys will be boys. That colt of yours has a strong right hook, I daresay. Speaking of colts . . ." He looked me up and down. I was still hot and tired from the race, but I tossed my head and kicked up my heels to show that I was far from winded.

"Embarr is coming three years old this season," Sir Henry said, "and I would like him to cover a few mares. He runs like a cheetah and jumps like a gazelle, but he's not acclimated to the rough terrain of this country. I am curious to see how he would cross with one of the local ponies. Unassuming creatures, they are, but full of spirit. So what say I let Embarr cover your mare—no fee, but as payment for a race well run?"

Mr. McKenna seemed surprised, but he agreed. While Liam led me up and down the street, seeming grateful to be apart from the merry crowd, Fiona appeared from the general store with a piece of rock candy. "A present from Mr. Beadle," she said as I crunched the treat. "He won three shillings on ye today!"

She glanced at Embarr on the far side of the town square. One of Sir Henry's men was sponging the mud from his legs, and another placed a scarlet cooler over his back. "He is a looker, though, isn't he?"

"But no match for our Darcy," said Liam, a bit of the old glint returning to his eyes.

That night, as I was nibbling grass under the stars, I saw a dark form lurching across the pasture. I shied and flared my nostrils until I caught Liam's familiar scent. I trotted over to him. He led me to the stone wall and laid his crutches against it, then slid carefully onto my back. His weight felt strange with one leg missing. Liam wrapped his fingers in my mane and clucked to me. Obediently, I stepped away from the wall.

After a quick circle around the stable yard, Liam leaned forward and signaled me to run. Although his seat felt different, his balance was still good. I was tired from my long ride that morning, but I arched my neck and galloped hard across the hills and valleys of my pasture, as if I were running the race all over again.

Afterward, Liam slipped down from my back and returned silently to the house. He still looked haggard and worn the next day, but I felt like something that was lost had returned to him. He came out to the barn with Fiona to see a new litter of kittens, and it seemed that his eyes were somehow more alive.

10

Berries and Briars

Sir Henry was true to his word, and I was bred to Embarr the following spring. For the first time I felt the stirring of new life as the foal grew inside me. Although it's said that Connemara ponies can survive on a thimbleful of oats and a bushel of thistles, the McKennas made sure that my belly was never empty after a long day in the field or at the shore.

I had always been bored by all the hitching-post gossip about foals that started up in early spring, but now I was as eager as anyone to speculate as to which mare would deliver a colt or a filly, or whether its color would take after the sire or the dam.

You're going to have a red colt, Darcy, said Mollie, Dr. Farber's mare, as we stood hitched outside the church one mild February day. *I can tell by the way your mane is split so it falls on both sides of your neck. A red colt, mark my words.*

Ach, you're full of old mares' tales, insisted Clover, a bay draft horse who pulled the town fire engine. *If Darcy was bred in the first week of April, it was a new moon in the sky. That means a filly, and it will be gray like herself.*

But they were both wrong, or perhaps each was half right. A month later, in the gray light before dawn, I gave birth to a black colt. I had never felt such pain before, but I forgot it as soon as my nose touched the wet, shivering creature in the grass. I licked him clean, and before the rooster crowed the colt was standing to nurse.

The children named him Finbarr, and for nearly a year he frolicked by my side. There was

no rest from the endless cycle of planting, hauling, and harvesting, and he learned to trot beside me as I pulled the cart or the plow.

The following spring, just before the seaweed harvest, I was brought to Hulton Manor to be bred to Embarr again. The stallion's ears pricked forward with interest when he saw Finbarr, his first colt.

What a handsome little fellow, he said. *He won't be as tall as me, but he's inherited your pretty face. I still say there's Arab in you somewhere.*

As snobbish as Embarr could be, there was no meanness in him, and I was glad to see him again. During the week that I stayed at the estate, I was treated royally. My stall was nearly bigger than the McKennas' cottage, and I breakfasted on grain sweetened with molasses and chopped apples. I had never tasted the likes of it before, and I fear I would have gotten quite fat had my visit lasted longer.

The whole time, Finbarr had been stabled in the stall across from mine. Although he no longer needed to nurse, I felt more at ease when he was within my sight. But when Mr. McKenna came to collect me, Finbarr remained in his stall. Once I was hitched to the pony cart, I whinnied and refused to leave the stable yard. Not without my colt!

Then Mr. McKenna did something he'd never done before: He slapped my haunches with the long whip he carried. Startled, I bolted out of the courtyard. Someone barred the door behind me, and I realized that Finbarr was no longer mine.

For weeks I was inconsolable. I would not eat the oats that Mr. McKenna put out for me, and I balked at the cart and plow. Mr. McKenna coaxed me gently, but when I still refused to walk on, he cracked me with the whip again. Furious, I did my work with my ears pinned flat against my head.

If I'd learned anything from my life on the farm, it was that every season will pass. Sometimes the most bitter disappointment can turn into the sweetest fortune. Mrs. McKenna had many wise old sayings, but her favorite was this: *What can come of the briar but the berry?*

If losing Finbarr was the briar, the berry was the new foal that was growing inside me. Now I understood why my dam had begun to push me away from her udder by the time the old farmer had sold me. She had to save her strength for the next foal. Slowly, my temperament returned to normal. The next spring, I delivered my second foal. Another colt, Torin, but this one was red like Embarr.

A few weeks after Torin was born, Shannon married a young doctor she had been courting. It is said that if a gray horse pulls a couple through town on their wedding day, the marriage will be a happy one. I hoped this was true as I carried Shannon and her new husband to their town house in Oughterard. I was sad to see Shannon depart, but I knew she was happy to leave the mud and hardship of a farmer's life. The Hultons even attended the wedding, and I daresay young Brendan's smile was a bit forced as he looked upon Shannon, who nearly glowed in her white dress.

The following year, to the chagrin of his father, Brendan joined the colonialist army in India. It was said that he cared nothing for politics, but only wanted the chance to shoot exotic animals and chase after foreign girls. Nobody missed the haughty lad, but I was regretful that he took Embarr with him.

Sir Henry was so pleased with Finbarr and Torin that he tried to buy me from the McKennas. But they refused, saying I was a member of the family. However, they made a deal with Sir Henry. In exchange for my next three foals, the family would be granted ownership of their farm. Now the McKennas would never have to answer to a moody landlord who thought they should have sown a bigger crop, or sell prized family keepsakes to make rent.

I delivered a filly and two more colts, all sired by one of the Hultons' stallions. Once my fifth foal was weaned, Mr. McKenna drove me over to the Hulton estate to sign the deed to the land. For the first time, I was able to see all of my foals together. They greeted me with elegant whinnies from their stalls in the stone courtyard. They had all grown sleek and strong. The younger colts were dappled gray like me, and the filly was dark bay with a coat as shiny as the polished wood of the carriage that she pulled for Sir Henry.

One by one, the other McKenna children left home to start lives of their own. Liam took a position at a telegraph station in New York City. A few years later, Tomas won a scholarship to a university in Dublin. Finally, he could read as many books as he wanted and not have to worry about milking the cow. As for Fiona, she went to work for the local veterinarian. Only little Connor remained. He was especially dear to the family because Mrs. McKenna had never been able to have another child.

Now Connor was a sturdy ten-year-old with hair like bleached summer straw. He was as fond of galloping across the countryside as his brothers and sisters had been, although these days I couldn't gallop quite as fast as I used to. My belly had grown a little bigger with each foal, and my silver-dappled coat had faded nearly to white.

One day Mr. McKenna drove me to the post office, hoping for a letter from one of the children, and instead found a notice from the Connemara Pony Breeders Society. The club had formed several years ago and held an annual show in Carna. All of my foals had won prizes there, and the society wished to register me as a foundation broodmare.

Soon after, a judge from the society came out

to the farm to inspect me. He was a distinguished-looking man in a tweed suit, and he seemed out of place on our little farm. I had been given a bath for the occasion, and Connor had spent hours brushing the burs and tangles out of my mane.

"The only thing harder than Connemara limestone is a Connemara pony's hooves," said the judge as he handled my feet.

After the inspection, weeks passed with no word from the society. I must not have measured up after all. But then, when I'd all but forgotten the incident, a package arrived. It was a certificate announcing that I was a purebred Connemara pony. There was also a blue ribbon attached, for the judge had inspected dozens of ponies in our region and found me to be the best.

Mr. McKenna hung the certificate and the ribbon in the barn, next to my bridle. I sometimes came into the barn just to look at them, although I felt a little silly. Blue ribbons didn't put turf in the shed or potatoes on the table. Still, it was nice to know that if I ever met Embarr again, I could casually mention that I was now a prize-winning, purebred Connemara pony.

Another decade passed this way—bearing foals, bringing in the turf, sowing and reaping the crops each season. Each time I was separated from one of my colts or fillies, my heart was broken anew. Each time it was mended by the birth of the next one.

At the age of twenty, my joints began to ache when I pulled a load of turf. Mr. McKenna noticed that I no longer seemed to take joy from my work.

That year the family did not sell my weanling filly, Aisling. They broke her to harness and built a larger stable for us. It was a joy to watch one of my foals grow up instead of surrendering her to a distant stranger.

The next spring I failed to catch with foal, and I knew my time as a mother had ended. Aisling, now three, had a foal of her own that year. A black filly. She reminded me of Ciara, and not only because of her coloring. Aisling's filly had the same fierce independence as my shadow sister from so long ago. She particularly delighted in teasing the new kittens, descendants of the fluffy creatures I'd met on my first day here, more than two decades ago. Had so much time really passed? The land seemed hardly changed, although the people on it had.

Mrs. McKenna's hair had gone pure white, and Mr. McKenna's hands were as knotted as an old tree branch. They trembled when he fastened the straps on my harness. At least he had help— Connor, now a strapping lad of eighteen, had decided to stay and tend the farm.

Today was Easter Sunday, and the family had just returned from church. Shannon and her husband had come for dinner with their three young children. The two boys and the flaxen-haired girl raced to the bottom of the hill where Aisling was nursing her filly.

Mrs. McKenna followed at a slower pace, wiping her soapy hands on her apron. She came over to where I stood and fed me a lump of white sugar. It dissolved quickly in my mouth, but left a lasting sweetness. We stood together, slitting our eyes against the wind as we watched the children playing with Aisling's foal.

"I believe ye understand better than anyone, sweet Darcy," said Mrs. McKenna, "the struggle to bear fruit in this unforgiving land."

I thought of the untamed coastal hills of my birth, and the crash of the sea's thunder. I recalled how Ciara used to nip me, then bolt away, over and over, until I followed her on whatever grand adventure she'd dreamed up. After all these years, I still remembered the piercing cry of the eagles on the cliff.

Thinking of times long past, I jumped in my skin as Shannon's little girl let out a shriek. The filly had stolen her Easter hat, then bolted away across the paddock. The wind blew the bonnet back over the filly's ears so that she appeared to be wearing the hat herself. But how beautiful she was, despite her silly antics. Black as a raven and twice as swift. In time she would turn gray, as I had, then cloud-wisp white. In time she would have foals of her own, although I knew I would never see this.

Despite the mild weather, I still felt the feverish pangs of my last labor in my belly. My joints were stiff, and food did not seem to nourish me as it once had. But looking out across the land on which I had toiled all these years, I felt no regret. The air was filled with laughter, and the sun was warm on my back.

APPENDIX

MORE ABOUT THE CONNEMARA PONY

Horses of the Emerald Isle

Horses were first brought to Ireland by the Celts around the fourth century. These were small, dun-colored animals prized for their hardiness.

In the twelfth century, Anglo-Norman soldiers invaded the country with their strong warhorses, adding size and substance to local stock. The refined Andalusians brought by Spanish traders in the 1600s helped create the sturdy yet beautiful ponies of the Connemara region on Ireland's western coast.

Early Connemara ponies were used for farming and transportation. They hauled turf, seaweed, and cartloads of the rocks that fill the fields of Ireland to this day. Trees were scarce near the coast, and most buildings were made of whitewashed stone. Ponies also pulled cartloads of the marsh plants used to thatch cottage roofs.

Connemara ponies were not the only equine breed in Ireland. Draft horses were often used for heavy farmwork. Irish drafts were crossed with

Thoroughbreds to produce the Irish Hunter, a horse usually kept by wealthy estate owners.

Most families could afford only one horse. The sturdiness and small size of the Connemara made it a practical choice for poor farmers who could not spare much extra feed for their livestock.

A Day at the Races

Irish country life wasn't all hard work. In a world before television, cars, cell phones, and computers, horse racing was a popular pastime for the poor and wealthy alike. Races were held over a turf course marked with flags. For many hardworking farmers, race days were an excuse to see friends, bet on their favorite ponies, and rest from the labors of the week. There were different races for mares and stallions, as well as a special race reserved for ponies under 13.2 hands. Men, women, and children could be jockeys in these informal meets. Due to the length of the course and the hilly terrain, the horses were out of the crowd's sight for much of the race, and a lot of rough riding took place. Jockeys tried to trip other horses and knock fellow riders out of the saddle. To win at an Irish track meet, a horse or pony had to be clever and agile as well as swift.

A New Breed

The Great Famine of 1845 to 1849 devastated the people of Ireland. Potatoes, originally brought to Europe from South America by the Spanish, had been imported from Spain in the late 1500s and became a staple food for the Irish people. When a fungus destroyed 90 percent of the potato crop, many families starved. Others were forced to emigrate to America or other parts of Europe, sometimes leaving young children behind with older relatives.

The horses of Ireland suffered as well, their number and quality greatly reduced by the famine. In the years that followed, the Congested Districts Board, formed to help alleviate poverty and overcrowding in western Ireland, imported Welsh cob, Thoroughbred, and New Forest pony stallions to help restore strength and vigor to the Connemara breed.

The Connemara Pony Breeders Society was formed in 1923. The ideal Connemara is 12.2 to 14.2 hands high, compact, and muscular, with a finely sculpted head and a gentle temperament.

The breed standard states that Connemara ponies should resemble miniature Thoroughbreds. Gray is the most common color, but Connemaras can also be bay, dun, black, roan, or chestnut. Pintos are not allowed into the registry.

The first Connemara to enter the studbook was a stallion named Cannon Ball, who reportedly won the Farmer's Race at Oughterard sixteen years in a row. Cannon Ball is said to have had a remarkable ability to find his way home from town while his owner slumbered in the cart behind him.

Connemaras Today

In recent years, the Connemara has become a popular mount for children and adults in the United States, Australia, and New Zealand. The breed is particularly noted for its jumping ability. The annual Connemara show in Clifden, Ireland, attracts hundreds of international visitors each year, many seeking to buy a genuine Connemara pony. Every Connemara must be inspected for conformation and soundness before it can be registered, ensuring the quality of the breed.

Famous Connemaras

In 1935, a twenty-two-year-old Connemara gelding called The Nugget successfully cleared a seven-foot, two-inch jump, a feat that few of the finest Thoroughbreds today would be capable of.

In the 1968 Olympics, a half-Connemara, half-Thoroughbred gelding named Stroller was one of only two horses in the competition to jump a clear round, with not a single rail fallen. Lendon Gray's half-Connemara, half-Thoroughbred gelding Seldom Seen was a prizewinning dressage horse despite being far smaller than most of his competition, standing only 14.2 hands.

The Connemara stallion Hideaway's Erin Go Bragh competed at the highest levels of three-day eventing in the 1990s. Erin Go Bragh has sired nearly two hundred foals, many of whom have become champions themselves, continuing the legacy of these tough and versatile ponies.

Horses of Irish Legend

Horses have been a part of Irish lore since ancient times. For example, there is a folk saying that if you break a mirror, bad luck can be averted by leading a horse through the house. And if you wear a braided lock from a black stallion's mane on your wrist, it will protect you from mischievous fairies.

Horses are important characters in Irish myths and stories as well. The pooka is a shape-shifting horse who lures people onto his back, then gives them the wildest ride of their life before throwing them off into a ditch. The dullahan is a head-less fairy that rides a fearsome black horse, and the kelpie is an equine water spirit that lurks in swamps, seeking to drown people. But not all of Ireland's mythical horses are malevolent. The Celtic goddess Rhiannon rides a shining white horse, and when a tempest breaks over the coast of Ireland, the whitecapped waves are said to be mystical sea horses.

About the Author

Whitney Sanderson is the daughter of Horse Diaries illustrator Ruth Sanderson. Her family has owned horses since she was a child, and her bookshelves were always filled with horse stories. Whitney owns an Appaloosa named Thor, who loves to go for trail rides in the New England woods.

About the Illustrator

Ruth Sanderson grew up with a love for horses. She has illustrated and retold many fairy tales and likes to feature horses in them whenever possible. Her book about a magical horse, *The Golden Mare, the Firebird, and the Magic Ring*, won the Texas Bluebonnet Award.

Ruth and her daughter have two horses, an Appaloosa named Thor and a quarter horse named Gabriel. She lives with her family in Massachusetts.

To find out more about her adventures with horses and the research she does to create Horse Diaries illustrations, visit her website, ruthsanderson.com.

Collect all the books in the
Horse Diaries series!

Eleská

Bell's Star

Koda

Maestoso Petra

Golden Sun

Yatimah

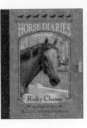

Risky Chance

Black Cloud

Tennessee Rose

Darcy

If you like the Horse Diaries, you'll love the Dog Diaries!

A puppy-mill dog's own tale

A guide dog who sees for her owner— and speaks for herself

Each book in the Dog Diaries series features a different dog who narrates a story that relates to its breed, training, history, or experience. From modern stories about puppy mill survivors—like *Ginger*—to historical stories about the first guide dogs—like *Buddy*—Dog Diaries combine compelling, fact-driven canine drama with the one thing kids most want to know about dogs: their inner-doggy dreams and desires!